Happy Birthday, Flora!

First published in 2010
by Wayland

Text copyright © Karen Wallace
Illustration copyright © Lisa Williams

Wayland
338 Euston Road
London NW1 3BH

Wayland Australia
Level 17/207 Kent Street
Sydney, NSW 2000

Series editor: Louise John
Editor: Katie Powell
Cover design: Paul Cherrill
Design: D.R.ink
Consultant: Shirley Bickler

A CIP catalogue record for this book is available from the British Library.

ISBN 9780750263207

Printed in China

Wayland is a division of Hachette Children's Books,
an Hachette UK Company

www.hachette.co.uk

Happy Birthday, Flora!

Written by Karen Wallace
Illustrated by Lisa Williams

WAYLAND

Characters

Flora: A shy elephant

Spots: A friendly leopard

Monty: A cheeky monkey

Lulu: A bossy parrot

Hilda: A happy hippo

Storyteller

Storyteller: Today is a special day in the Jungle. It's Flora's birthday. Monty the monkey has decided to play a trick on Flora.

Storyteller: Hilda, Lulu and Spots are eating breakfast when Monty swings through the trees to join them.

6

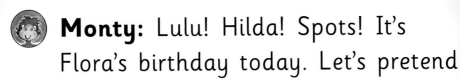 **Monty:** Lulu! Hilda! Spots! It's Flora's birthday today. Let's pretend we've forgotten all about it.

 **Spots:** Why would we do that? It's mean!

7

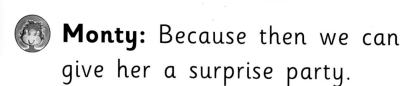 **Monty:** Because then we can give her a surprise party.

 **Spots:** That's a great idea, Monty!

Hilda: Where shall we hide her presents?

Lulu: By the river. We can have the party there, too!

Storyteller: Everyone is excited about the party. Suddenly, Monty thinks of a problem.

Monty: How will we get Flora to the river?

Hilda: I could ask her to come swimming with me.

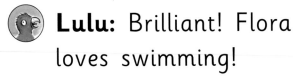 **Lulu:** Brilliant! Flora
loves swimming!

Spots: Lulu, Monty and I will get
the party ready. Hilda, you go
and keep Flora busy for now.

Storyteller: Hilda finds Flora sitting on a log, eating her breakfast.

Hilda: Hello, Flora.

12

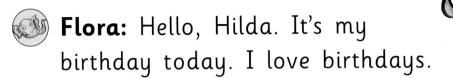 **Flora:** Hello, Hilda. It's my birthday today. I love birthdays.

 **Hilda:** Happy birthday! What are you going to do today?

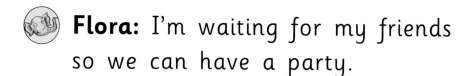 **Flora:** I'm waiting for my friends so we can have a party.

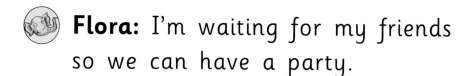 **Hilda:** I can't see Monty, Lulu or Spots. Do you think they have forgotten your birthday?

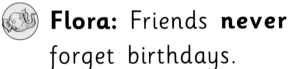 **Flora:** Friends **never** forget birthdays.

Storyteller: Flora looks everywhere for her friends.

Flora: Look, here they are!

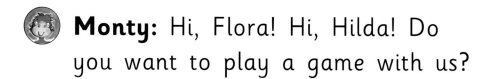 **Monty:** Hi, Flora! Hi, Hilda! Do you want to play a game with us?

Spots: Let's play 'I Spy'. I spy with my little eye something beginning with 'p'.

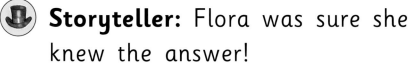 **Storyteller:** Flora was sure she knew the answer!

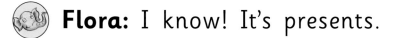 **Flora:** I know! It's presents.

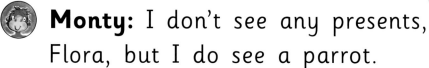 **Monty:** I don't see any presents, Flora, but I do see a parrot.

 **Lulu:** It's my turn to choose a game now. I want to play 'Hide and Seek'.

18

Spots: Flora, you're 'IT'!

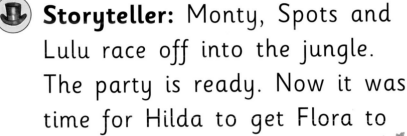 **Storyteller:** Monty, Spots and Lulu race off into the jungle. The party is ready. Now it was time for Hilda to get Flora to the river.

19

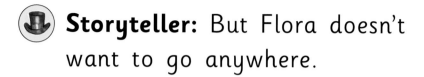 **Storyteller:** But Flora doesn't want to go anywhere.

 **Flora:** My friends **have** forgotten my birthday.

20

Hilda: Don't cry, Flora. I know what will cheer you up.

Flora: Nothing will. This is the **worst** birthday I've ever had!

21

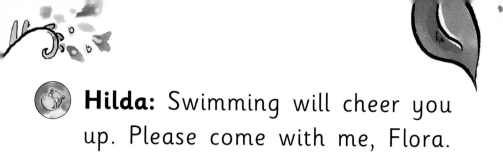

Hilda: Swimming will cheer you up. Please come with me, Flora.

Flora: No, I don't want to.

Hilda: Please, Flora. It'll be fun.

Flora: Well, I suppose I haven't got anything else to do. OK, I'll come. I do like swimming.

Storyteller: Flora and Hilda set off through the jungle.

24

Hilda: Look, Flora. I can see balloons!

Flora: Balloons? Where?

Hilda: By the river. Come on!

Storyteller: Flora and Hilda race through the jungle.

Flora: We're nearly there. Maybe my friends have remembered after all.

26

Storyteller: And Flora was right! Monty, Spots and Lulu were waiting by the river.

27

Monty, Spots and Lulu: Surprise!

Storyteller: Flora couldn't believe her eyes! There was a big cake and a **big** pile of presents.

28

Monty, Lulu, Spots and Hilda: Happy birthday, Flora!

 Flora: This is the **best** birthday ever! TOOOOOOOOOT!

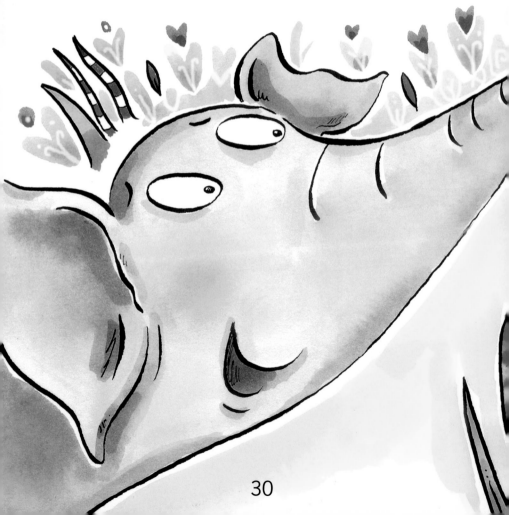

START READING is a series of highly enjoyable books for beginner readers. **The books have been carefully graded to match the Book Bands widely used in schools.** This enables readers to be sure they choose books that match their own reading ability.

Look out for the Band colour on the book in our Start Reading logo.

The Bands are:

Pink Band 1A & 1B

Red Band 2

Yellow Band 3

Blue Band 4

Green Band 5

Orange Band 6

Turquoise Band 7

Purple Band 8

Gold Band 9

START READING books can be read independently or shared with an adult. They promote the enjoyment of reading through satisfying stories, plays and non-fiction narratives, which are supported by fun illustrations and photographs.

Karen Wallace was brought up in a log cabin in Canada. She has written lots of different books for children, fiction and non-fiction, and even won a few awards. Karen likes writing funny books because she can laugh at her own jokes! She has two sons and two cats. The sons have grown up and left home but the cats are still around.

Lisa Williams did her first drawing at 15 months old - it was a worm! She told her mum to write 'Worm' underneath the picture. When she was five, she decided that she wanted to be an illustrator when she grew up. She has always loved drawing animals and hopes that you will enjoy this book...